Look and Find

The
Wizard
of Oz

Illustrated by Bob Terrio

Cover illustrated by Ernie Colon

Illustration Assistants: Gale Terrio and Joan Terrio

Illustration script development by David Martino

Louis Weber, C.E.O.
Publications International, Ltd.
7373 North Cicero Avenue
Lincolnwood, Illinois 60646

Manufactured in the U.S.A.

8 7 6 5 4 3 2 1

ISBN 0-7853-0066-X

Look & Find is a trademark of
Publications International, Ltd.

PUBLICATIONS INTERNATIONAL, LTD.

Dorothy and her little dog Toto were swept off the Kansas prairie by an unexpected cyclone. Twisting and turning in their uprooted house, they wondered if they would ever land.

Dorothy and Toto weren't the only things going 'round and 'round. Can you find these other spinning things?

A record

A ballerina

A lasso

An electric fan

A basketball

A pinwheel

An eggbeater

A globe

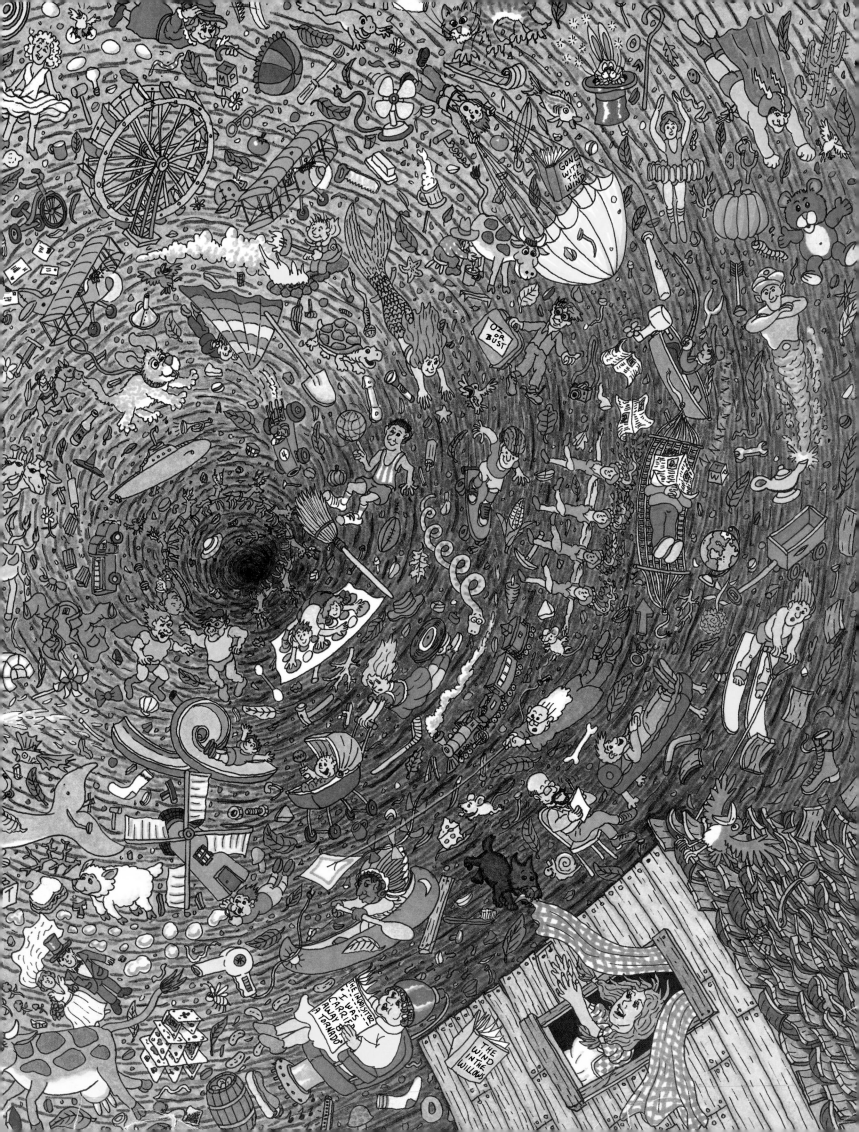

Dorothy's house landed with a THUMP! When she stepped out, little people called Munchkins welcomed Dorothy to their beautiful land. They also told her about the witches who ruled the other side of the rainbow.

Can you find Dorothy and Toto? Can you find these citizens of Munchkin Land?

Dorothy

Toto

Jim Shorts

Mini Pearl

Tiny Tim

I. M. Lyttle

Chick N. Little

The Good Witch of the North

The Good Witch of the North told Dorothy to follow the yellow brick road to the Emerald City. There, the Wizard of Oz might help her find a way home. The Scarecrow, Tin Woodman, and Lion said they would go, too.

Dorothy and her friends lost some things on the way to the Emerald City. Can you find them?

Dorothy's ribbon

The Tin Woodman's oil can

The Scarecrow's sneakers

The Cowardly Lion's crown

Toto's bone

The Queen of the Field Mice's dinner

The Good Witch's wand

Having locked on their green glasses, Dorothy and her friends entered the Emerald City and headed for the Palace of Oz. The Wizard of Oz refused to grant their wishes until they could destroy the Wicked Witch of the West!

Take a look around the Emerald City with *your* green glasses. Do you see these green things?

This lucky leprechaun

Broccoli

This snake

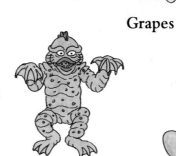

This caterpillar

Grapes

Pistachio ice cream

The Creature from the Green Lagoon

A frog prince

On their way to the castle of the Wicked Witch of the West, Dorothy and her friends were beset by fearsome wolves, bees, Winkies, winged monkeys, and other creatures who served the Wicked Witch.

Can you find these dangerous creatures who tried to capture Dorothy and her friends?

"Wolf"gang Amadeus Mozart

Don Coyote and Sancho Panther

"Owl" Capone

Ludwig Von "Bee"thoven

Wee Willie "Winkie"

The Big Bad Wolf

"Crow" Magnon

Wing Ed Monkey

Dorothy was captured by the Wicked Witch. But when the Wicked Witch tried to steal one of Dorothy's silver shoes, Dorothy angrily splashed her with a bucket of water. The Wicked Witch melted away!

Can you find these witchy guests who are visiting the Wicked Witch's castle?

Harriet Hex

Baby Batwing

Hannah Hexecutive

Granny Graves

Dr. Vibes

Hagatha Hepplewhite

Lady Isabel Newton

Enchantra Pavlova

Dorothy was reunited with her friends. Together they went back to Oz to claim their promised prizes. But the Wizard of Oz was not really a wizard! He was just an ordinary man with many clever disguises.

Look for the Wizard of Oz, then look for these costumes and disguises in his throne room.

A fright wig

The Wizard of Oz

A makeup kit

Fake wings

A Viking hat

This scary mask

Elevator shoes

This silly mask

A magician's cape

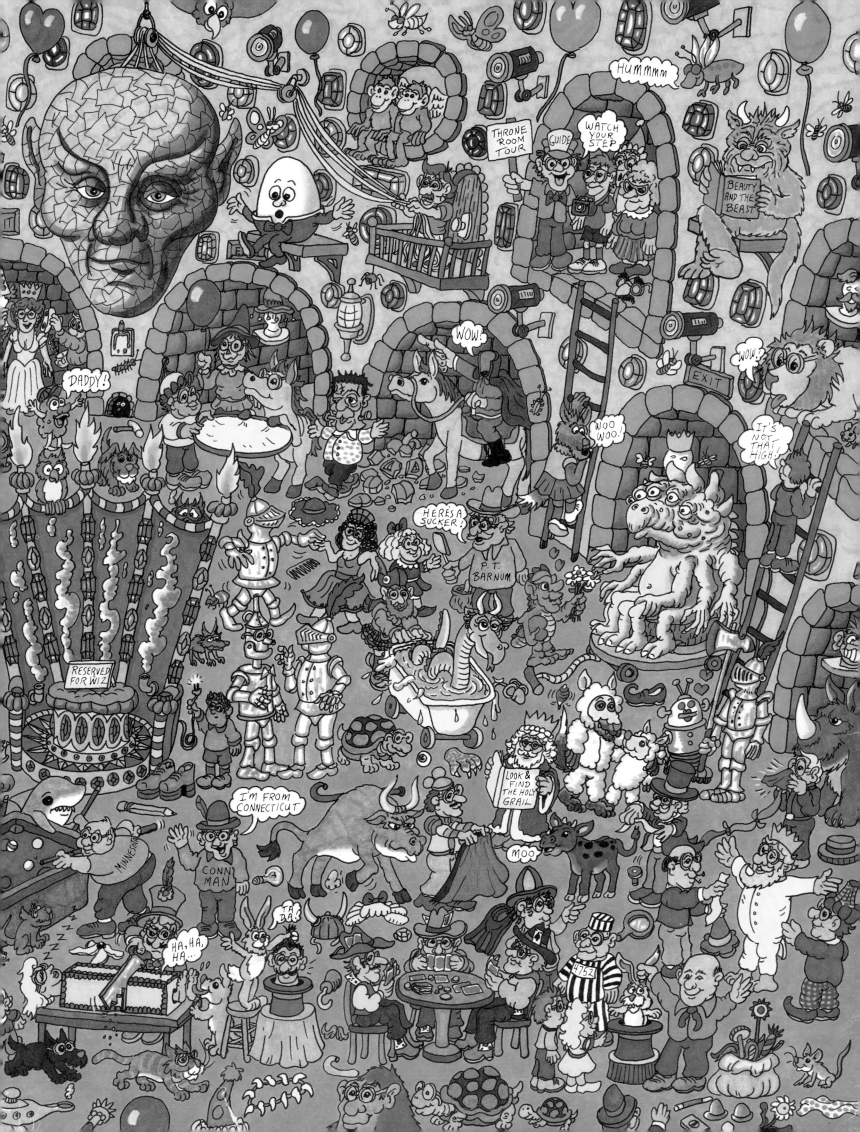

W hen the Wizard of Oz left without her, Dorothy decided to find the Good Witch of the South and ask for her help. Dorothy and her companions traveled through the Dainty China Country where everything was of made porcelain or glass.

Can you find these tiny citizens of the Dainty China Country?

Frau Jill

Auntie Dainty

Dolly Kitt

Mr. I. Glass

Sir Ammick

Redd China

Chip Dent

Ol' Doc Crockery

Portia Lynn

At last, Dorothy found Glinda the Good Witch living among the Quadlings in a *very* red country. Glinda told Dorothy that a simple click, click, click of her silver heels would send her home. With tearful good-byes, Dorothy left her friends with the Good Witch.

How quickly can you find these "quazy" Quadlings?

Quaptain Queeg

Queen Quertsy

Quentin Quark

Dr. Quincy Quadling

Quathy Quick

Quinn Quombings

The Quadling Quints

Quasimodo Quadling